A NOTE TO PARENTS

When your children are ready to "step into reading," giving them the right books—and lots of them—is as crucial as giving them the right food to eat. **Step into Reading Books** present exciting stories and information reinforced with lively, colorful illustrations that make learning to read fun, satisfying, and worthwhile. They are priced so that acquiring an entire library of them is affordable. And they are beginning readers with an important difference—they're written on four levels.

Step 1 Books, with their very large type and extremely simple vocabulary, have been created for the very youngest readers. **Step 2 Books** are both longer and slightly more difficult. **Step 3 Books,** written to mid-second-grade reading levels, are for the child who has acquired even greater reading skills. **Step 4 Books** offer exciting nonfiction for the increasingly proficient reader.

Children develop at different ages. **Step into Reading Books,** with their four levels of reading, are designed to help children become good—and interested—readers *faster*. The grade levels assigned to the four steps—preschool through grade 1 for Step 1, grades 1 through 3 for Step 2, grades 2 and 3 for Step 3, and grades 2 through 4 for Step 4—are intended only as guides. Some children move through all four steps very rapidly; others climb the steps over a period of several years. These books will help your child "step into reading" in style!

For my prince,
Willie De Vries
—D. H.

Random House 🏠 New York

Text copyright © 1992 by Random House, Inc. Illustrations copyright © 1992 by Carolyn Ewing.
All rights reserved under International and Pan-American Copyright Conventions. Published in the
United States by Random House, Inc., New York, and simultaneously in Canada by Random
House of Canada Limited, Toronto.

Library of Congress Cataloging-in-Publication Data:
Hautzig, Deborah.
The Nutcracker ballet / retold by Deborah Hautzig / illustrated by Carolyn Ewing.   p.   cm. —
(Step into reading. A Step 2 book) Summary: A little girl helps break the spell on her toy
nutcracker and changes him into a handsome prince. ISBN 0-679-82385-9 (trade)
— ISBN 0-679-92385-3 (lib. bdg.) [1. Fairy tales.] I. Ewing, C. S., ill. II. Title. III. Series.
PZ8.H2944Nu 1992   [E]—dc20   92-3320

Manufactured in the United States of America
17   18   19   20

STEP INTO READING is a trademark of Random House, Inc.

Step into Reading

THE NUTCRACKER BALLET

Retold by Deborah Hautzig
Illustrated by Carolyn Ewing

A Step 2 Book

It was Christmas Eve.

Marie and her brother Fritz

peeked into the living room.

"Oh, I can't wait for the party

to start!" said Marie.

At last the living room doors were opened,
and the children rushed in.

The Christmas tree was dazzling!

Hundreds of tiny candles twinkled.

Sparkling decorations and candies

hung from all the branches.

Under the tree were so many presents!

Soon the guests arrived.

Aunts, uncles, cousins, and friends

came carrying even more presents.

Marie ran to greet her godfather.

He was an odd-looking man.

He was tall and thin.

He wore a black patch over one eye

and a frizzy white wig on his head.

He looked magical and spooky.

But he was a wonderful godfather.

He always came with amazing toys

that he had invented himself.

This Christmas Eve he came with
a big red box and a bigger green box.
He opened the red box and out stepped
a very big toy soldier.
Godfather turned the key on his back—
CRANK! CRANK! CRANK!

The soldier marched around the room!

Left, right, left, right.

As the key turned,

he marched slower and slower.

Then he jerked to a stop.

Next Godfather opened the green box

and wound up two toy clowns.

They danced together!

Everyone clapped in delight.

Then Godfather looked under the tree.

He picked up his present for Marie

and gave it to her.

It was a wooden nutcracker

shaped like a little man.

Marie knew at once that

the nutcracker was special.

His legs were too short.

His head was too big.

He wore a fine purple suit

with brass buttons.

On his head was a funny little hat.

His eyes were kind and gentle.

He had a white beard

and a wonderful smile.

Godfather watched Marie
with a twinkle in his eye.
"It is a small gift," he said to her.
Marie hugged the nutcracker
and said, "It is the present I love
best of all."

Then Fritz grabbed

the nutcracker from Marie.

"What an ugly fellow!" he said.

He ran across the room.

Marie ran after him.

Fritz put the biggest walnut
into poor Nutcracker's mouth.
CRACK! CRACK! CRACK!
Three little wooden teeth fell out.

"Stop it, Fritz! You're hurting him!"
cried Marie.

She took the nutcracker back
and rocked him in her arms.

"I will protect you,"
she whispered. "Forever!"

After the party was over

and everyone was in bed,

Marie could not sleep.

She tiptoed downstairs

into the dark living room.

It was so, so quiet…

and then…

BONG! BONG! The grandfather clock

began striking midnight.

Marie was surprised by the noise.

She looked up at the tall clock,

and suddenly she saw

something strange at the top.

Something that was moving.

Godfather was sitting

on top of the clock!

He peered down at Marie

like an owl.

"Godfather, you scared me!" cried Marie.

But before she could say

another word,

the most amazing thing happened.

The Christmas tree began to grow.

It grew bigger

and bigger—

and bigger.

As the Christmas tree grew,

the windows and toys

and everything in the room

grew with it.

Soon the toys

were the same size as Marie!

Marie watched in amazement.

Suddenly she heard:

"SQUEAK! SQUEAK! SQUEAK!"

Then she heard the pitter-patter

of many feet.

Dozens of tiny eyes
glittered and darted all around her.
Marie was surrounded
by an army of huge mice!

Out jumped the King of Mice.

He had seven horrible heads,

each with a golden crown.

He took out his sword

and glared at Marie.

"Where is Nutcracker?" he hissed.

Marie would not tell him.

The King of Mice squeaked

his command to his army.

"Find Nutcracker!"

The door of the toy chest

flew open.

Out popped toy soldiers, puppets, and dolls.

They were led by Nutcracker.

Now he was the same size as Marie.

Drums beat! Trumpets blared!

The battle began.

He was leading the army of toys!

Swords clashed! Cannons boomed!

Nutcracker's army chased the mice.

But more and more mice came.

Nutcracker's army of toys was being beaten.

Mice surrounded Nutcracker.

The King of Mice

grabbed Nutcracker's sword.

"Now I have you!"

he squeaked.

Marie watched in horror.

"Oh, my poor nutcracker!"

she cried.

What could she do?

She kicked her right shoe

as hard as she could

at the King of Mice.

POOF! Like magic,
the mice were gone.
Every single one.

Marie turned to look

at the nutcracker she loved.

And before her eyes

the funny-looking wooden nutcracker

became a handsome prince.

He looked at Marie

with his kind eyes

and his wonderful smile.

"You saved my life.

Now let me take you

to my kingdom—

the Land of Sweets!"

The prince led Marie

out the window

and into Christmas Wood.

The snowflakes tasted like sugar,

and little snow fairies

danced all around them.

Soon they came to the prince's palace.

A beautiful lady greeted them.

"She is the Sugar Plum Fairy,"

the prince told Marie.

"And now—to the party!"

Marie and the prince

went into the palace.

They sat together

on a golden throne

in a crystal room.

All the people

in the Land of Sweets appeared.

One by one they performed

their special dances

for the prince and Marie.

From Spain came the dance
of hot chocolate.

An Arabian lady

did the dance of coffee.

Chinese dancers jumped

out of a giant teapot

and did a lively dance.

From Russia came

the dancing candy canes.

From France came Mother Ginger

and her little puppets.

They ran out

from under her skirt

and did a playful dance.

Then all the flowers

of the kingdom

danced the Waltz of the Flowers.

"I wish we could stay here forever!"
Marie said.

"Yes," said the prince.

"But now it is time to go on
to other wonderful places!"

Marie and her nutcracker prince
stepped into the royal sled
and waved good-bye.
The sled rose slowly into the sky.
Marie and the prince
she had loved from the start
vanished from sight.